The Bee and the Venus Flytrap

Om KIDZ
An imprint of Om Books International

First Published in 2023

Om Kidz | Om Books International

Corporate & Editorial Office
A-12, Sector 64, Noida 201 301
Uttar Pradesh, India
Phone: +91 120 477 4100
Email: editorial@ombooks.com
Website: www.ombooksinternational.com

Sales Office
107, Ansari Road, Darya Ganj
New Delhi 110 002, India
Phone: +91 11 4000 9000
Email: sales@ombooks.com

ISBN: 978-93-94547-21-6

Printed in India

10 9 8 7 6 5 4 3 2 1

The Bee and the Venus Flytrap

I'm all set to read

Paste your photograph here

My name is

Busy Bee was always **very** busy. He **never** had a break.

He had to visit at least fifteen hundred **flowers** in a day.

In the summertime,
Busy Bee visited **flowers**
with his **cousin,** Silly Bee.

Silly Bee **laughed** all the time. Sometimes she **danced** on top of the **flowers, making** even **them laugh!**

One day, while **buzzing** through the warm air, Busy Bee saw a curious new **flower** in the neighbourhood.

This new **flower** looked strange. It was not tall **like** the other **plants.**

Its **leaves** looked **like** two lips. Small hair **grew** along the outer edges of the **leaves.**

The **bee** had **never** seen anything **like this plant.** Inside, it glowed in a purplish red.

Busy Bee wanted to **make friends with this plant.** But he felt scared.

Meanwhile, Silly Bee came to **hang** around **with** Busy Bee. When she saw the **flower,** she said, "Look at that **plant with** funny-shaped **leaves!**

A hairy **flower,** that's **hair-**larious!"
And Silly Bee did what she did so often… she **giggled** at her own jokes.

Suddenly, Silly Bee bumbled **into** the centre of the **leaves.** It was cosy in there like on a comfortable **chair.** She **said,** "I can see you're new here! If you get bored, ask for me, and I'll cheer you up with a joke!"

At once, the odd **leaves** of **this** new **plant** closed **very** fast around Silly Bee**, trapping** her inside. A sticky **juice** began to pour out of the **leaf walls.**

Silly Bee's **legs were** trapped. She couldn't move the smallest bit.

“Good Lord!” shouted Busy Bee in panic. Why **were** the mean **leaves** trapping his **cousin**? Was **this** the dangerous **plant which** ate **insects** and **bugs?**

Meanwhile, Silly Bee took a deep breath and tried to **wriggle** out. But she was truly stuck.

Busy Bee got **very** angry.
He flew over to the mean **plant** and started **banging** on the closed **leaves.**

"Hey, you, Mrs new-flower-in-town, let go of my **cousin** at once! **What** do you think you're doing?"

The **leaves** of the Venus Flytrap opened up. It was trying to **catch** Busy Bee. But Busy Bee was too fast for it!

The **leaves** snapped shut. Now Busy Bee **jumped** up and down on the bouncy **flower like** on a **trampoline.**

As soon as the insect-eating **flower** opened up, Busy Bee **pulled** Silly Bee out! The head of the Venus Flytrap had opened and shut quickly too **many** times.

The **plant** lost all its strength and fell to the ground.

"You saved my life, **cousin!** This **plant** was trying to eat me alive!" said Silly Bee. Busy Bee smiled. It was great to **have** his **little cousin** back.

All the other **bees** of their hive **danced** and **sang** around **them with** joy.

Know Your Words

Sight Words

have	make	them	what
into	many	this	which
like	never	very	with
little	said	were	

Naming Words

bee	flower	juice	plants
bugs	friends	leaf	trampoline
chair	hair	leaves	walls
cousin	insects	legs	

Doing Words

banging	giggled	laughed	trapping
buzzing	grew	making	wriggle
catch	hang	pulled	
danced	jumped	sang	